Wolfpack Gang is Outta Sight!

By Reese Everett

Illustrated by Sally Garland

Rourke
Educational Media
rourkeeducationalmedia.com

www.rourkeeducationalmedia.com

Edited by: Keli Sipperley
Cover layout by: Renee Brady
Interior layout by: Rhea Magaro
Cover and Interior Illustrations by: Sally Garland

Library of Congress PCN Data

Wolfpack Gang is Outta Sight! / Reese Everett
 (Rourke's Beginning Chapter Books)
 ISBN (hard cover)(alk. paper) 978-1-63430-375-0
 ISBN (soft cover) 978-1-63430-475-7
 ISBN (e-Book) 978-1-63430-571-6
 Library of Congress Control Number: 2015933732

Printed in the United States of America,
Conover, North Carolina

Dear Parents and Teachers:

Realistic fiction is ideal for readers transitioning from picture books to chapter books. In Rourke's Beginning Chapter Books, young readers will meet characters that are just like them. They will be drawn in by the familiar settings of school and home and the familiar themes of sports, friendship, feelings, and family. Young readers will relate to the characters as they experience the ups and downs of growing up. At this level, making connections with characters is key to developing reading comprehension.

Rourke's Beginning Chapter Books offer simple narratives organized into short chapters with some illustrations to support transitional readers. The short, simple sentences help readers build the needed stamina to conquer longer chapter books.

Whether young readers are reading the books independently or you are reading with them, engaging with them after they have read the book is still important. We've included several activities at the end of each book to make this both fun and educational.

By exposing young readers to beginning chapter books, you are setting them up to succeed in reading!

Enjoy,
Rourke Educational Media

Table of Contents

1
No Girls Allowed

My name is Deano and I like to dance and play soccer. But did you know sometimes kids will make rules like "No girls allowed"? At my old school we did not have that rule. But today is my first day at Windy Pines Elementary. Apparently, it's a different ballgame at this place.

At recess, some boys in my class chose teams. I stood on the side waiting to be picked. They started the game before anyone picked me. I stood and watched a while. I kicked the dirt. I asked Miss Booker for another ball but there was only one. I kicked the dirt some more. Some girls in my class asked me if I could do cartwheels. I can do cartwheels so I did one. But I wanted to play soccer, so I did not do more than that.

"What's so funny?" Tommy asked me.

"Nothing," I said. I looked down at the ground because I felt shy for a minute. Then I said, "Can I play?"

"No girls allowed," he said.

"Fine!" I huffed. I kicked the dirt again. Then I saw a boy sitting at a picnic table. A dog sat next to his feet. I didn't know you could bring your pets to school! The dog was black and its fur was poofy. I thought it needed a haircut. The boy also had black poofy hair. He wore darkers. That's what we call sunglasses in Jamaica. He ran his fingers on the page of a book.

I wanted to pet that fluffy dog so I walked over to the table.

"What are you reading?" I asked him. "And how come your dog is allowed at school. Can I pet him?"

He did not stop tracing the page with his fingers. He also did not look at me. "No, you can't pet him," he said.

"Why do you want to play with the stinky boys?" a girl named Vern asked me.

"I just want to," I said. She looked at me like I had seven heads.

Tommy scored and his team cheered. I wanted to cheer but also I wanted to cry. My friends at my other school always wanted me on their team. I was the best goal scorer in second grade!

I missed my old school. This morning, Miss Booker asked me to tell the other boys and girls a little about myself. I said I was from Jamaica and that bulla cake is my favorite. Some of the kids laughed and said "Bulla, bulla!" like it was a funny word. They also did not know where Jamaica is. Miss Booker got out a map and showed everyone. I wished I could jump into the map and go back there.

Tommy's team scored again. A boy named Cojo said "Whoop, whoop!" It sounded silly so I laughed a little.

I looked at his book. It had a lot of bumps on the page like someone had messed up the paper. And also there were pictures of people playing ball! I said a *Whoop, whoop!* in my head.

"What is wrong with your book?" I asked. "Why can't I pet him?"

"It's Braille," he said. "And Sully is my service dog."

"What's that?" I said. I'd never heard of Braille. And what did service dog even mean?

The boy turned toward me. "I'm blind," he said. "Braille lets me read with my fingers. Sully helps me get places." He moved his fingers on the page again. I think he wanted me to go away. But I didn't, because this was the coolest thing I'd ever heard.

"So you can't see me at all?" I asked.

"Nope," he said. I stuck my tongue out. I wagged my fingers in front of my face. I wiggled my shoulders. He did not do anything.

"Is it hard to read like that?" I asked.

"Not for me," he said.

Miss Booker called out that it was time to go back to class. I got up and stuck my tongue out at the boy one more time.

"What's your name?" I asked him.

He got up, too. So did Sully.

"Jay," he said.

He started walking toward the class. To my class!

"Are you in Room 220?" I asked. He was not in there this morning. I would have noticed that fluffy dog.

"Yes." He stopped and turned toward me. "Are you?"

"Yes!" I said. "I'm new. Where were you before?"

"I had to go to the doctor for a physical," he said.

"Oh, because of your eyes?" I asked.

"No, because I had to get a checkup for the new season," he said.

I did not have time to ask him what that meant because Miss Booker made us zip lips and walk single file. I tried to walk with my eyes closed. I bumped into Vern.

"Ow," she said.

Oops.

2
Reading
Fingers

It turned out that Jay and Sully sat at the table next to mine. Even though I couldn't pet Sully, it was fun to have a dog in class.

Jay was quiet but also nice. No one else in Room 220 talked to him much. But I did. Miss Booker said *Shhhh* to me. But I kept talking. I had lots of questions.

"What is it like?"

"Have you ever been able to see?"

"How did you learn to read with your fingers?"

Jay said *Shhhh* to me too. But then he smiled.

"I was born blind," he said. "I learned to read Braille way back in preschool."

I felt sad for him.

"It must stink to not be able to play stuff," I said.

Miss Booker called everyone to the front of the room. I sat right next to Jay and Sully on the carpet. My hands itched to pet Sully so I sat on them. But then I thought, *he can't see me!* so I reached over to touch him. Miss Booker saw me and said, "No."

She gave me the stink eye. I tucked my hands back under my legs fast.

Miss Booker read a story about a dragon and a girl named Perry that could do tricks. Then we brainstormed a new story together. Everyone called out their ideas.

"There's a monster that eats basketballs," Cojo said.

"It's afraid of bunny rabbits," Marwa said. She wiggled and jumped up and down. "Ooh, ooh, but only purple ones!"

"It collects calculators and someone stole one!" Tommy said.

I raised my hand.

"Yes, Deano?" Miss Booker said.

"The monster is a soccer player but no one will let her play because she is a girl," I said.

Tommy laughed at that. His glasses slid down his nose. He pushed them back up and stuck his tongue out at me. I made a scowling face at him.

Miss Booker wrote our ideas all over the white board. It looked like a big mess of words. Then she told us to go back to our seats and put the ideas together in a story.

I closed my eyes and wrote some stuff. Then I opened them. I couldn't read any of it.

I wondered how Jay was going to do his work since he couldn't see. But Miss Booker sat next to him and read the ideas from the white board. Then he used a special typewriter to write his story.

I wanted to read it but my fingers don't know how to read.

3 Who's the Boss?

I told Mom and Dad all about Jay and Sully when I got home from school. I also told them about the stinky boys who made the rules for soccer at recess. I was not happy with those guys.

"What makes them the bosses, anyway?" I grumped.

Momma pulled me over for a squeeze. She felt smushy and warm. "They are not the bosses, Deano," she said. "You just gotta show 'em what you're made of."

I am made of skin and bones and Bulla cake, I told her. She laughed.

"Tomorrow is a new day," she said. "Maybe some of the other girls in class will want to play soccer with you."

"I wish Jay could play soccer," I said. It made my belly hurt to think he couldn't do things like that. It wasn't fair.

"Who says he can't?" Daddy said.

I grabbed a soccer ball and went out to the front yard. I tried to kick it around with my eyes closed. Daddy came out and kicked the ball with me. Momma came out, too. She was a star player back in the olden days. They tried closing their eyes, too. We ran into each other a few times. Once, I kicked Daddy in the leg on accident. Also, sometimes I peeked.

When I decided to make a big play, I squeezed my eyes shut and kicked hard where I thought the ball was. Whoosh! There was nothing but air. I lost my balance and fell on my butt.

I heard a loud laugh.

"Nice move," a boy's voice called. Tommy and Jose stopped their bikes in front of my house. They laughed some more then pedaled away.

"I had my eyes closed!" I yelled at them. They didn't turn around.

"Those boys stink," I grumbled.

"I think they think you stink, too," Daddy laughed.

"That's not funny, mister," I grumped.

"It is, only because you don't," he said.

I knew what he meant. But it didn't make it any better.

4
Hungry like a Wolf

My second day at Windy Pines started as a disaster. I ripped my pants and spilled paint all over the place before we even had morning snack. Sully tried to lick the paint. Miss Booker's face looked like she was trying not to be grumpy about the mess.

"Sorry," I said to her. She patted my hand and said not to worry. Then she gave me a pin to close up the rip in my pants. That made Tommy and some other boys laugh. I made a noise like a growl when Miss Booker wasn't listening.

"Are you a wolf, Deano?" Tommy said. "Jay is a wolf, aren't you, Jay?" He made a howling sound. Miss Booker told him to simmer down.

Miss Booker said a special guest would be coming in class before recess. I sort of hoped it would be a dragon. And that it would eat Tommy.

"Is it a police officer? Will there be snacks?" Vern asked. Then she shot her arm up in the air like she remembered that part too late.

"No, it is not a police officer," Miss Booker said.

"Is it a zookeeper?" Krisney asked. He did not bother raising his hand. Miss Booker did not answer him because of that.

"Yes, Marwa?" she said instead.

Marwa put her hand back down. "Um, I forgot."

Miss Booker smiled with one side of her mouth. "Anyone else have a guess?"

"Is it a calculator salesman?" Tommy asked. That boy sure like calculators.

Miss Booker laughed a big HA HA HA!

"No, it is not a calculator salesman," she said. Tommy looked disappointed. I was glad it wasn't a calculator salesman because that sounded boring.

The rest of the class took turns guessing. I got into the game, too.

"Is it a ghostbuster?" I asked. I squeezed my hands together like I was praying. A ghostbuster would be the coolest.

Miss Booker shook her head and laughed again. "Nope," she said. Bummer, I thought. But also I was happy I made Miss Booker laugh. She was a pretty nice teacher.

Then, out of nowhere, Sully sat up and barked. Loud. I hadn't heard that dog make a peep before. It made me jump.

"Whoa!" Tommy said. "That dog CAN bark."

Our classroom door opened. A man walked in. He was the tallest person I'd ever seen. His legs and arms were covered in dark hair. A red bag was slung over his shoulder. It looked heavy. And lumpy.

"Hello, everyone," he said. His voice sounded like thunder booming.

"Hello," the class said together.

"This is Mr. Wolf," our teacher said.

I was a little bit scared because he looked like a wolfman. What if he ate Tommy AND the rest of us?

Then he walked over to Jay and Sully. He patted Sully on the head. I let out a gasp and waited for him to get in trouble. But then he hugged Jay. I was so confused!

"Mr. Wolf is Jay's dad," Miss Booker said. "He's going to teach us some new things. Doesn't that sound fun?"

Everyone nodded. I was still afraid he might eat us.

"Can you see, Mr. Wolf?" Marwa asked.

He laughed. His laugh sounded like booming thunder, too.

"Yes, I can see," he said. "But pretty soon, you won't be able to." He smiled a funny smile.

Oh, no, I thought. I do not like this at all. I looked at Jay but his face wasn't saying anything. He didn't tell me his dad was a wolfman. I wasn't sure we could actually be friends now.

I was sorry I wanted a dragon to eat Tommy. Even if he is mean. Now I just hoped we both would survive this special guest.

5
Bells and Whistles

Miss Booker told us to come sit at the front of the room. She gave Mr. Wolf her chair. He looked funny when he sat down, like a giant in a baby seat.

Jay and Sully sat next to him, facing us. Jay bit his lip and cracked his knuckles. He looked scared. Or maybe excited. I couldn't tell. Mr. Wolf cleared his throat. He pulled out a whistle that was tucked in his shirt. Then he pulled a hat out of his bag and put it on his head. It said COACH.

"Does everyone like to play games?" he asked us.

I nodded. Some people said "Yes." One boy said "No." Mom would say he was trying to be difficult.

Mr. Wolf pointed at me. "What kind of games do you like to play?"

I sat up straight and put on my serious face. "Soccer is my favorite," I said.

Tommy poked Krisney in the side. They both laughed. Miss Booker shot them a look.

"I like video games," Vern said. She pretended she was pushing buttons on a controller. Then she fell over on the carpet for a second.

Miss Booker said, "Sit up, Vern."

"I like to play football with my brothers," Marwa said.

"Those are all fun games. Jay here has been playing sports since he was in diapers. But the rules and equipment are a little different," Mr. Wolf said.

Vern giggled. So did I, but just a little. Because thinking about Jay in diapers was sort of funny. Then I looked at the wolfman and hoped the game wasn't dangerous. What if Jay was a wolfboy and he wanted to eat us all, too?

I stared at Jay. He didn't look like a wolf. His hair was poofy but he didn't have sharp teeth. Then I decided if he was a wolfboy, he would still be my friend. Because he could read with his fingers and that is almost like a superpower.

Mr. Wolf asked Miss Booker to turn down the lights. Then he pushed a button on the TV remote. Suddenly, the screen was full of kids playing soccer. I clapped my hands together. Then I stopped because I wasn't sure if clapping was allowed.

"Watch them play," Mr. Wolf said. "Does anything look different?"

Everyone watched. No one said anything. I could not see anything different. Then, Mr. Wolf said, "Listen." He turned up the TV volume as high as it would go.

"What's that jingling sound?" I asked.

"Great ears, Deano," Mr. Wolf said. "That is a bell inside the ball. All of the players are blind."

"WHOA!" Tommy said.

"That's crazy!" Krisney said.

Just then, a player in the video made a sweet goal. "Whoop, whoop!" I said. I clapped my hands over my mouth but Miss Booker cheered, too.

"That was Jay winning the game," Mr. Wolf said. His face looked proud. He did not look scary to me anymore. He just looked like a regular dad. An extra-large dad.

I looked at Jay. He was smiling so big I could count his teeth. But I didn't, because counting teeth is boring. Instead I asked, "Can we see that again?"

Mr. Wolf replayed the goal. This time, he slowed down the video.

Jay's kick was AWESOME!

6
No Boys Allowed

Mr. Wolf told us all about coaching Jay's soccer team. Jay answered lots of questions from the class. He talked like he couldn't get the words out fast enough. Sully seemed excited too. He sat up and licked Jay's face. That made us laugh.

They also talked about another game we'd never heard of. Its name was goalball.

"In goalball, three players line up on each side. Then they try to get the ball into the other team's zone. The ball has a bell in it so you can hear it coming," Mr. Wolf said. "But you have to listen carefully."

"Can we play goalball?" Krisney asked. "And soccer, too?"

The answer was YES! We went outside to the playground. Mr. Wolf told us to warm up by racing around the swing set and crossing the monkey bars. We all ran our fastest. Sully and Jay led the pack. Then we gathered around Mr. Wolf.

"Jay will be one team captain," Miss Booker said. "And Krisney will be the other."

"I want to be on Jay's team," Tommy said.

Jay laughed at that. "No boys allowed!" he said.

I turned to Tommy and smiled. But not a mean smile. Just a HA HA smile. Because that's what he gets for being a stinky rule maker.

And guess what happened then? Jay picked me FIRST. I let out a Woot, Woot! then went to stand by him. Krisney picked all boys. Jay picked all the girls. He gave me a fist bump when our team was together.

"What's our team called?" Marwa asked.

"The Wolfpack Gang!" I said. Jay smiled.

"Yes!" everyone agreed. We put our hands together and said "Go, Wolfpack!" like a real professional team.

"Just one more thing before we get started," Mr. Wolf said. He pulled a small bag out of the big lumpy bag. Then he opened it and said,

"Everyone take one."

We reached in the bag and pulled out long pieces of fabric.

Blindfolds!

7
Bulla, Bulla!

Goalball was trickier than it sounded. Especially because we couldn't see! Mr. Wolf also gave us goggles to wear over our blindfolds. This was to protect our eyes, he said. Once I lifted my blindfold a little bit. Then I felt like a cheater pants so I didn't do it again.

We took turns playing different positions. The only way to find the ball was to listen for it. Sometimes my ears played tricks on me. I went the wrong way. Once I crashed into Marwa. It made us both laugh.

We kept playing goalball till both teams scored six points. Miss Booker liked a tie game, she said. But Mr. Wolf said there would be no tie in the soccer game. He pulled a trophy out of his lumpy bag and set it on the table. "This game is for the Windy Pines Cup," he said.

I looked at the trophy. Then I looked at Tommy. He was looking at the trophy, too. Then he looked at me.

"You're going down, mister," I said. But not in a mean way. Just in a fun way. Because mostly I was just happy to play. But also I wanted to win.

"No way," he said. Then he ran over to his team and huddled up.

Jay called our team over for a huddle, too. A huddle is when you put your heads together and talk about your game plan. Our game plan was to score a lot of goals. But to do that, we had to talk to each other, Jay said.

"Make sure you tell us where you are," he said. "And listen for the ball."

The only people on the teams who would be able to see were the goalies. We chose Vern to play in the net for us. Krisney's team named Cojo its goalkeeper.

My stomach did excited flip flops. I went out to the center of the field and pulled the blindfold back down over my eyes. I listened for Mr. Wolf to blow the whistle.

"WREEEEEE!" The sound of the whistle made my feet move. I couldn't see, but I could feel the ball at my toes. I heard Jay say, "Over here!" Then I kicked it toward his voice.

"Over here," I heard Marwa say. I jogged up the field, trying to hear everything. And also trying to not trip. I could hear other players breathing. I also could sense they were close, even though I couldn't see them.

I heard the ball coming toward me. Then I heard Jay say, "Take it, Deano!" I listened for the sound then I got the ball between my feet and dribbled it a little ways. Then I said, "Your ball, Jay!"

"Here!" he said. I passed the ball toward his voice. I heard him call for Marwa. Then I heard a SWOOSH from the ball. And an UMPH from Cojo. And a "GOAL!" from Miss Booker.

The Wolfpack Gang cheered for Marwa. Then we settled down and lined up at center again. Krisney's team kicked off. Jay got the ball and led our team straight to the net.

And guess what! I scored!

I wanted to do that over and over! But Krisney's team had figured things out. I could hear them yelling to each other more. Then they scored on Vern.

Tommy did a Whoop, whoop! Krisney did a BOO-YAH!

I said, "Nice goal," even though I didn't actually see it.

I didn't want them to score any more goals. I clenched my teeth real tight and tried to concentrate on my team's voices. When I got the ball, I tried to take it all the way down the field.

Bad idea. Krisney stole the ball and passed it down toward our net. Then they scored again.

It was a tie game. Time was running out. Jay called us over.

"This is it, Wolfpack," he said. "Let's get 'em!" We cheered and cheered and high fived. Except we couldn't see so mostly we put our hands in the air. I accidentally smacked Marwa in the head.

"Sorry," I said.

We went back out to center field. I got to do the kickoff. "All yours, Jay!" I yelled.

I kicked the ball toward him, then followed the sound of the ball down the field. I heard the other team saying "Over here, over here!" But no one could keep up with Jay.

Ring a ling a ling! The bell inside the ball tinkled. It *ring a ling a ling*-ed all the way to the net.

"GOAL!" Miss Booker yelled.

"Game over," Mr. Wolf said, blowing his whistle as the timer beeped for end of the second half.

I took off my blindfold and high fived my team. I was so excited. And also sweaty.

"You're not bad for a girl," Tommy said to me. I gave him a fist bump.

"You're not bad for a boy," I said.

The Wolfpack Gang gathered around the trophy for a picture. Then Jay and I carried it

back to class with Sully leading the way.

"I'm on Jay's team at recess tomorrow!" Tommy said.

"Me too!" I said.

"Me three!" Vern said.

"Who's hungry?" Miss Booker asked. "I brought bulla cake for snack time!"

My mouth opened huge. Miss Booker winked at me.

"Bulla, bulla!" The class laughed.

"Bulla, bulla!" I laughed, too.

Reflection

Being the new kid at school can be sort of
scary. There's a lot of things to figure out,
like where the restroom is and what time
you get to have a snack. There's also the
tricky part of making friends. I was sad
when the boys wouldn't let me play soccer
with them on the playground just because
I'm a girl. I was also a little sad when I
met Jay. I thought he couldn't do anything
because of his blindness. Then I figured out
he could do all kinds of cool things. And
he helped the other boys in class see that
anyone can play sports. Go Wolfpack!

Discussion Questions

1. Why did Deano feel left out on the playground on her first day at Windy Pines?

2. What was Jay doing when Deano first noticed him?

3. Why do you think Sully could not be petted?

4. Why was Deano scared of Mr. Wolf at first?

5. Have you ever been told you couldn't play a game because you are a boy or a girl? How did that make you feel?

Vocabulary

Can you use each of these words in a sentence? Can you turn those sentences into a story of your own?

blindfold
Braille
brainstorm
controller
gasp
goalball
huddle
trophy

Writing Prompt

Close your eyes and listen to the sounds around you. Can you tell what is going on without being able to see? Write about what you heard. Describe the sounds and what made them.

Q & A with Author Reese Everett

Did you play soccer as a kid?
I did not play soccer when I was growing up, but I wish I had! I was always the last kid picked for teams at PE and recess. It made me think I wasn't good enough to play sports. Now, as an adult, I am trying new activities and learning to play the games I felt left out of as a kid.

Have you ever seen a blind soccer game?
I have! My children and I were watching TV one day and we came across a blind soccer game. We were fascinated with the way it works. We started talking about what it might be like to not be able to see. Then we gathered up some gear and headed to the park to try it out. We split up into teams and tried to keep our eyes closed the whole time. There was a lot of laughing but not a lot of goal scoring. It gave me an enormous amount of appreciation for the talented athletes who play this game.

Make Your Own Bulla Cake

Ingredients:

4 cups flour

¼ cup water

1 teaspoon baking powder

1 cup dark sugar

½ teaspoon baking soda

4 oz. butter, melted

¼ teaspoon salt

2 teaspoons vanilla

1 teaspoon cinnamon powder

1 tablespoon molasses

½ teaspoon nutmeg, grated

3 tablespoons ginger, grated

½ teaspoon cloves, ground

Directions:

Preheat oven to 350 degrees. Grease baking sheet. Sift flour, baking powder, baking soda, salt, cinnamon, nutmeg, and cloves. Mix water, sugar, melted butter, ginger, vanilla and molasses in a jar. Combine dry mixture and liquid to make a dough. Dust a rolling pin and board with flour. Flatten the dough to make it 1/8 inch thick. Cut dough into 4-inch circles. Place on baking sheet and bake for 25 minutes. Cool and serve.

Websites to Visit

www.pbskids.org/arthur/print/braille
http://braillebug.afb.org
www.timeforkids.com/news/
goalball/39381

About the Author

Reese Everett is a children's book author from Tampa, Florida. She loves her four kids, silly adventures, and sunny days at the beach. And avocados. Her favorite thing to see is people being kind and helpful to others.

About the Illustrator

Sally Anne Garland
was born in Hereford
England and moved to
the Highlands of Scotland
at the age of three. She
studied Illustration at
Edinburgh College of Art
before moving to Glasgow where she now
lives with her partner and young son.